It Came from Beneath the Bed!

Other Bunnicula Books by James Howe:

Bunnicula (with Deborah Howe)
Howliday Inn
The Celery Stalks at Midnight
Nighty-Nightmare
Return to Howliday Inn
Bunnicula Strikes Again!

James Howe is the author of the award-winning bestseller, *Bunnicula,* and its sequels, as well as many other popular books for young readers, including *The Misfits* and the Pinky and Rex series for younger readers. He lives in Hastings-on-Hudson, New York.

TALES FROM THE HOUSE OF BUNNICULA

BUNNICULA

It Came from Beneath the Bed!

JAMES HOWE

ILLUSTRATED BY BRETT HELQUIST

SCHOLASTIC INC.

New York Toronto London Auckland Sydney
Mexico City New Delhi Hong Kong Buenos Aires

ISBN 0-439-52480-6

12 11 10 9 8 7 6 5 4 ?   3 4 5 6 7 8/0

Printed in the U.S.A.   40

First Scholastic printing, February 2003

Book design by Ann Bobco
The text of this book is set in Berkeley.
The illustrations were rendered in acrylics and oils.

To Alex Anest, who once let me hold his pet tarantula—
and to Jessie, Florrie, and Chris
— J. H.

For Mary Jane
— B. H.

HOWIE'S WRITING JOURNAL

Uncle Harold—who is a dog, like me, and not even my uncle, I just call him that—got me this real cool notebook from under Pete's bed. Pete is not a dog. He's one of the two boys who lives in our house. Since he isn't exactly what you'd call neat, a lot of stuff ends up under his bed. Uncle Harold said Pete would never notice the missing notebook. So now it's mine.

I want to be a writer just like Uncle Harold. Uncle Harold has written all these books about Bunnicula, this strange but lovable rabbit who lives here with us. "Us" is the Monroes—Mr. and Mrs. Monroe and Toby and Pete and Uncle Harold and me, and, of course, Pop, this totally awesome cat whose real name is Chester. I call him Pop. In my personal opinion, Pop is the coolest thing since chew bones.

I don't want to write about real-life stuff the way Uncle Harold does, like Pop trying to kill Bunnicula because he thinks he's a vampire or the time we stayed at this boarding kennel and there were talking bones buried there, because if I stick to real stuff like that it'll just be boring and I'll never get to use my imagination. When I asked Uncle Harold what I could write about, he said it sometimes helps to start with something you know and see where it takes you.

Well, being a wirehaired dachshund and all, one thing I know about is the floor. I could write a story called "The Floor."

Or not.

I also know about water dishes and food

dishes. I could write "The War between the Water Dish and the Food Dish." That's it! That's what I'll write! See, there's this water dish that's always crying because it thinks the dog, who happens to be this really cool wirehaired dachshund puppy, likes the food dish better and . . .

What a dorky idea.

Do all writers have this much trouble?

Hmm. Let's see.

Uncle Harold isn't the only one who spends time under Pete's bed. I do, too. It's really dark under there. It smells like Pete's totally gross sneakers, and there's dust and all kinds of junk and food so old it's got whiskers.

(It doesn't really have whiskers. That's what's called "literary license," which means when you're the writer you can pretty much say whatever you want. I don't know why it's called a license, since it's not like writers have to wear tags or anything. I'll have to ask Pop. He knows everything.)

Now where was I?

Under Pete's bed. That's it! I know what my first story will be!

It Came from Beneath the Bed!

By Howie Monroe

CHAPTER 1:
"THE SCARY PLACE"

Pete Monroe was a slob. He did things like sneak food into his room and instead of sharing it with his pets like any decent human being would do, he would toss what he didn't want under his bed. Sometimes the pets, especially the cute and lively wirehaired dachshund puppy named Howie, would go under the bed and look for something good to eat.

But under Pete's bed was a scary place. It was dark and full of secrets.

"Do not go there!" Chester the cat (who is sometimes called Pop, but won't be in this story because it's too confusing) warned Howie, the frisky and clever puppy. "You might not come out alive!"

"Ha, ha!" Howie retorted cleverly.

"Go ahead and laugh!" Chester said. "But don't say I didn't warn you!"

Howie bit his tongue to stop himself from saying, "I didn't warn you."

Even though Howie told Chester, "Ha, ha!," he didn't really mean it. That is because he believed what Chester told him. Chester knew a lot of stuff and Howie thought he was the coolest thing since chew bones.

Soon Howie was scared to go back under that bed. The only way he could prove that there was nothing *really* to be frightened of was to go under the bed in the dark of night. When the moon was full.

He did not know why it was important for the moon to be full, but in scary stories whenever people—or puppies—go into haunted houses, they do it on nights when the moon is full.

Howie, who was adorable, kind, and witty, had many friends in his neighborhood. He decided that he should ask one of his many friends to go with him under Pete's bed the next time the moon was full.

Most of them did not want to go with him.

"Beware!" they told him, their voices trembling with fear.

"Be there or be square," he told them back.

But they didn't care if they were square. Not one of them. Well, okay, one of them.

That one was Delilah, a puppy who had recently moved in down the street. Delilah was beautiful, but not too smart.

(Delilah, when you read this, remember: It is ONLY A STORY!!!!!)

"I'll go with you!" Delilah said.

They waited until Pete was sound asleep.

"What's *that*? What's *that*?" Delilah kept asking when she wasn't bumping her head. (When she was bumping her head, she said, "Ow, ow, ow," instead.)

But when she wouldn't stop, Howie, whose keen eyes and powers of observation were second only to those of the legendary detective Sherlock Holmes, told her what each thing was.

"That's a balled-up soccer shirt and that's half a baloney sandwich that was stale *last* week and that's the remote control Mr. Monroe has been looking for and that's Pete's homework he couldn't find yesterday and that's Pudgykins."

"Pudgykins?" asked Delilah.

"Pete's koala bear he's had since he was two that he keeps under the bed for emergency hugs and thinks nobody knows about."

"Awww," said Delilah. "That's sweet."

"Sweet, harrumph," said Howie, the manly yet sensitive dachshund puppy.

"And what are all those things?"

Howie sniffed at the things and sneezed. "Dust bunnies," he said.

"EEK!!" screamed Delilah as she scrambled out from under the bed. "Dust bunnies! Dust bunnies! Run for your lives!"

Howie's Writing Journal

Uncle Harold read what I wrote and said that it's a GOOD BEGINNING!!!!!!

I asked him if he would send it to his publisher for me and he said maybe I should write the rest of the story first.

Rats.

He also said that he thinks something exciting should happen soon. I said, "What about the dust bunnies?"

He said he doesn't think most readers will
be excited about dust bunnies.

So now I have to think of something
REEEEEEEALLLLLLY EXCITING!

CHAPTER 2:
"THE ATTACK OF THE GIANT SQUID!!!!"

That night, there was a TERRIBLE storm!!!! The Monroes were awakened by a HORRIBLE *screeching* sound that was followed by these *ka-phlumph* noises like GIANT SUCTION CUPS being attached to the house!!!!

Mr. Monroe looked out the window!!!! "GIANT SUCTION CUPS are being attached to the house!!!!" he cried in alarm.

15

Everyone *SCREAMED!!!!*

The house was being *attacked* by a GIANT SQUID that had risen from the waters of Lake Erie to *DESTROY* Planet Earth!!!! The Monroes went running into the night in their *pajamas!!!!* The house was flattened and Pete fainted from *SQUID BREATH!!!!* It looked like he was a goner until Howie, the courageous and plucky dachshund puppy, *put his own life at risk* by going back and

Howie's Writing Journal

Uncle Harold said maybe it doesn't have to be <u>that</u> exciting.

And besides which, the squid comes out of nowhere and that's cheating.

I said, "But Uncle Harold, the squid didn't come out of nowhere. It came out of Lake Erie!"

He rolled his eyes (I don't know why) and

said, "I mean, the _idea_ of the squid comes out of nowhere. You just put the squid in for excitement. You need to put something in that connects to the rest of the story."

I guess he's right.

He also said I might be using too many adjectives, especially when describing one of the characters.

I have no idea what he's talking about.

CHAPTER 3:
"THE SCIENCE EXPERIMENT"

The next day, the ever curious and bouncy Howie scampered up the stairs and down the hall to Pete's bedroom.

He was stopped by a sign on the door that read:

DO NOT ENTER
SCIENCE EXPERIMENT IN PROGRESS
FUMES MAY BE FATAL

KEEP OUT
that means you!

Just then, Pete's brother, Toby, walked by Howie and pushed open Pete's door.

"Can't you read?!" Howie heard Pete shout.

"You're not doing any science experiment," said Toby. "Unless you call seeing how long you can lie on your bed without doing your homework a science experiment."

"I *will* be doing a science experiment!" Pete shot back.

Later that night, when most of the house was asleep, Howie heard a strange noise coming from upstairs. As he got closer to Pete's room, the noises got louder. And there was the strangest smell. . . .

Howie, the alert and inquisitive dachshund puppy, poked his nose through the half-open door.

What he saw stopped him *dead in his tracks!!!!*

(That is just an expression. Howie did not die and he also did not have dirty paws.)

The room was filled with test tubes gurgling with strange-colored liquids. Streams of smoke rose up and filled the room like ghosts. In a graveyard. On Halloween. Pete sat hunched over his desk, mumbling to himself.

Howie perked up his keen ears and listened carefully.

"If I can only perfect this formula," Pete was saying, "I'll have what every eleven-year-old boy dreams of: world domination and an A in science!"

He threw back his head and cackled wildly.

Howie could hardly believe his ears. He knew that Pete sometimes acted like he was one kibble short of a full meal, but could he really be out to dominate the world? How would he do that, anyway? He didn't even have a driver's license. He'd have to get his parents to drive him everywhere. What if they didn't want to? And if he was busy dominating the world, wouldn't he miss a lot of school?

Howie could not help feeling sorry for Pete as he imagined him flunking out of sixth grade and having to dominate the world without a high-school diploma.

But that feeling didn't last long.

"What are *you* doing here?!" he heard Pete hiss accusingly. "Get out!"

Pete jumped up from his chair and waved his arms frantically.

"Not a word of this to anyone, do you hear me, dog? If I find out that you've been squealing . . ."

The demented boy put his hands to his own throat and made a choking sound.

Howie scampered out of the room as fast as you could say, "Pete Monroe's gone bonkers!"

Even faster.

(NOTE: In case Pete ever reads this: NONE OF THIS REALLY HAPPENED! I am making it all up in order for the story to be as exciting as a giant squid!!!!)

CHAPTER 4:
"THE POTION"

That night, Howie had terrible dreams.
Over and over, Pete appeared out of nowhere,
his hands outstretched, hissing, "I'm going to
get you, squealer! You're dead meat!"

Waking up in a sweat, Howie vowed not to
tell anyone what he had found out, not even
Chester.

The next morning, he told Delilah.

"You have to promise not to tell anyone
what I'm about to tell you," he said.

"Okay," she replied, "but does it have anything to do with . . . with . . . oh, you know."

"No," said Howie, "I do not know."

"With . . . with . . . oh, it's too horrible to say . . . I can't . . . but I must, I can't live tormented by my fears . . . with . . . with . . . *d-d-dust b-bunnies?!!!*"

Howie, being a deep-thinking and perceptive dachshund puppy, concluded that the subject of dust bunnies was an upsetting one to Delilah, especially seeing as how she had just fainted.

"There, there," Howie said as he revived Delilah. He had never noticed before that she had eyelashes. And what lovely eyelashes they were. "You'll be all right. I'll never let those bunnies harm you."

"Oh, Howie," Delilah said, batting the eye-lashes he had not known until a moment before even existed, "you are so manly yet sensitive."

He was almost ashamed to tell her his dream. But he needn't have feared. In Delilah's eyes, he could do no wrong.

"You have to stop him!" Delilah said. "You can't let him whatever-you-said-he-was-going-to-do."

"Dominate the world."

"Yeah, that. And I'm going to help you."

"No, Delilah, it isn't safe."

"But I can't let you go alone. I'd never forgive myself if something happened to you."

Howie looked into Delilah's eyes. He saw himself reflected there. He *was* a cute puppy.

He could understand why Delilah felt the way she did. "Well, okay," he told her.

So that night, Howie and Delilah returned to Pete's room. They hid under the bed and waited.

Howie had gone back under the bed earlier in the day and cleaned out all the dust bunnies with his tail. He also found two Oreo cookies, one of which he ate then and there, and the other of which he waited to share with Delilah.

She liked the filling. He liked the cookie. They were meant for each other.

"What are we waiting for?" Delilah asked after they had finished eating the Oreo.

The intelligent and smart, not to mention wise, dachshund puppy gave Delilah's question serious consideration. "I'm not sure," he told her at last, "but we'll know when we find out."

Howie could feel the breeze coming off Delilah's fluttering eyelashes.

"You are so intelligent and smart," she told him. She did not mention wise.

As it turned out, they did not have long to wait.

They scurried farther back under the bed as they heard Pete enter, close the door, and sit down at his desk.

Soon the room was filled with the gurgles and stench of science gone mad.

"That's it!" they heard Pete cry. "I have the answer at last!"

"I didn't hear the question," Delilah whispered in Howie's ear.

"That tickles," replied Howie, whose every sense was as finely tuned as a concert piano.

"Yes!!!!" Pete exclaimed to no one (or so he thought). "No more homework! No more having to clear the table! With this potion, I will be more powerful than anyone on the face of the Earth. Even Ms. Kipper! Ya-ha-ha-ha!!!!"

Later, after Pete had gone to sleep and Howie had explained to Delilah that Ms. Kipper was Pete's school principal, the two dogs crept out from under the bed.

"We must find that potion and destroy it!" Howie told Delilah.

"But look!" Delilah said.

One of the test tubes was missing! Where could it be?

Delilah gasped. "There!" she cried.

"Where?" said Howie.

"There!" she cried. Again.

"Oh, no!" said Howie, the strong and determined yet capable-of-being-surprised dachshund puppy. "How will we get the potion now?"

There, clutched in Pete's sleeping hands, was the vile vial, filled with purple ooze.

Howie said, "We're doomed."

Delilah said, "Being doomed makes me hungry."

"Me, too," said Howie.

They went downstairs and had something to eat.

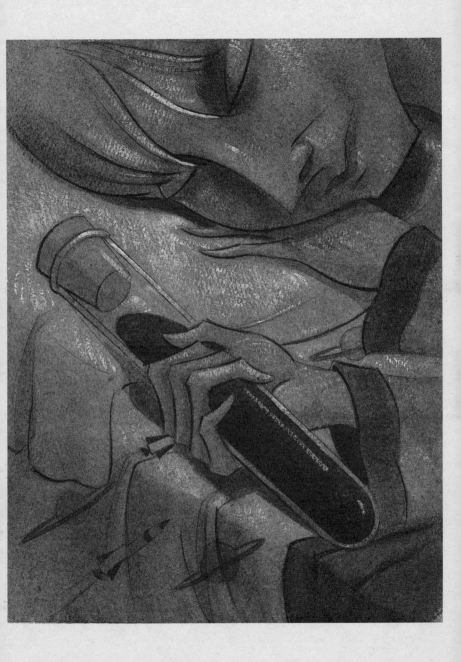

HOWIE'S WRITING JOURNAL

Uncle Harold said this is STRONG WRIT-
ING!!!! He liked the part about the "vile vial"
and said that "every sense was as finely
tuned as a concert piano" was an excellent
simile.

Whatever that is.

But he said the last chapter ending fell
flat. He said I should try using a cliff-
hanger, which is when you leave the reader

wondering what's going to happen next.

I told him, "But the reader doesn't know what Delilah and Howie had to eat."

He said that for him that <u>was</u> a cliff-hanger, but he guessed that the average reader might be looking for something a little more mysterious than what's in the food bowl.

I'll try again.

Delilah gasped. "There!" she cried.

"Where?" said Howie.

"There!" she cried. Again.

"Oh, no!" said Howie, the strong and determined yet capable-of-being-surprised dachshund puppy. "How will we get the potion now?"

There, clutched in Pete's sleeping hands, was the vile vial, filled with purple ooze.

Howie said, "We're doomed."

Delilah said, "Being doomed makes me hungry."

"We can't think of our stomachs at a time like this," said Howie. "We've got to save the world."

"Okay," said Delilah. "But then can we get something to eat?"

"Okay," said Howie.

He raised himself on his hind paws and peered at the sleeping boy. Inching his finely shaped head forward, he opened his professionally trained jaws, ready to secure the test tube in their grasp. Soon the world would be safe from harm and he and Delilah could go downstairs and get something to eat.

Then . . . *disaster struck!!!!*

HOWIE'S WRITING JOURNAL

Cliff-hangers are awesome!!!!!

Uncle Harold asked, "What's the disaster?"

I said, "You'll have to read the next chapter to find out!"

He said, "Well, let me read it."

I said, "I have to write it first."

Writing is awesome!!!!!

CHAPTER 5:
"DISASTER!"

Pete suddenly swung his arm in the air.

Startled, Howie thought, *He must be dreaming about baseball again.*

The test tube flew out of Pete's hand and landed in the space between the bed and the wall.

"You'll never get it now," Delilah fretted.

"I've got to go in and give it a try," the square-shouldered, iron-jawed, wirehaired dachshund said, dropping down to all fours and looking Delilah in the eyes.

"Oh, but you *mustn't,* you *mustn't,* I beg you," Delilah whimpered, tossing her curly blonde ears from side to side. "I know this mission is important, I know the fate of the whole world is at stake, but why do *you* have to be the one to go in? Why now . . . now, when we've only just met? We have our whole future ahead of us, our whole past behind us, our whole present, um, *with* us. Please, Howie, think of the children."

"Children?" Howie asked. "What children?"

"*Our* children," Delilah cried. "The children we'll one day have if only you *don't* go."

"I'm just a puppy," said Howie. "I'm too young to think about having children. Besides, there's a job to be done and I've got to do it!"

"Then let me go with you," Delilah insisted.

"No," the heroic and protective Howie replied. "You stay here, where it's safe and doesn't smell."

Delilah stifled a sob as the valiant Howie crawled under the bed. The foul aroma of aging socks hit his nostrils like a finely tuned concert piano.

It was dark under there, so dark it hurt, and smelly, not just from the socks but from sneakers that should have been retired a year ago and moldering food and mildewed comic books and . . .

That's when he saw it—the stain of purple creeping down the wall! The stopper had come out of the test tube! All the liquid had run out! Whatever that formula was, it was no longer safely contained. It was out in the

world now, where Pete alone knew what harm it might cause. But Pete wasn't even aware that the spill had taken place. He was snoring loudly, muttering in his sleep about strikes and foul balls.

Wearily, Howie crept out from under the bed.

Delilah was there with a picnic basket and an American flag. "I waited for you, Johnny," she told him.

"My name is Howie," he reminded her.

"Oh, but you're safe at home now," she said. "The dust bunnies didn't get you, that's all that matters."

Howie told her about the formula dripping down the wall.

"Is that bad?" she asked.

"It's not good," Howie told her.

"What are we going to do?"

"Nothing."

"Nothing? But—"

"Nothing," Howie said in the firm yet affectionate tone she had come to see as manly yet sensitive.

There was nothing left they *could* do. Nothing anybody could do.

Nothing.

Except pray.

Howie's Writing Journal

Writing stinks!!!!!!!

It gets you in trouble!

I let Delilah read what I wrote and now she's not speaking to me!

She said I'm making her sound stupid and that her character is an insult to females everywhere and what is that business with the picnic basket and American flag, anyway?

I tried to explain. I said, "In a story like

this, the man is always the hero and the woman gets to admire him."

I think that's when she stopped speaking to me.

And what does she have against the American flag?! She said it didn't make sense and I said it didn't have to, because I have a literary license!!!! She snatched the doggie treat I was eating right out of my mouth and said I wouldn't have room for it because I was TOO FULL OF MYSELF!!!!

Maybe _that_ was when she stopped speaking to me.

Is it my fault that Delilah doesn't understand the way stories work?

I thought she'd at least like what I wrote
about her eyelashes.

CHAPTER 6:
"THE TERRIBLE THING UNDER THE BED!"

The next morning, Howie found a note from Delilah under the mat outside the front door of the Monroes' house.

"I have fallen in love with someone else," it read. "I cannot see you anymore. Please do not come sniffing around my yard. Good luck with saving the world."

A tear fell from Howie's manly yet sensitive cheek.

Just then, he heard a cry far greater than the one his heart was silently screaming inside his chest. He ran up the stairs to Pete's bedroom.

"No, no, no!" Pete was crying.

"What is it?" Mr. Monroe, Pete's father, called in alarm as he rushed into the room, almost stepping on the adorable yet low-lying dachshund puppy. "Are you okay, Pete?"

"Uh, er, uh, yeah, I'm okay," said Pete. "I just uh, er, uh, lost my science homework."

Pete's father shook his head. "Why don't you look under your bed?" he asked. "That's where everything else ends up."

"Ha, ha," Pete laughed. "Okay, Dad."

As soon as Mr. Monroe left the room, Pete scrambled under the bed. The clever and quick-thinking Howie hid himself behind the bunched-up sleeping bag that was still next to Pete's bed from the time his friend Kyle had stayed over two weeks ago.

"Whew," he heard Pete say. "No harm done. But I don't know if I'll ever be able to duplicate that formula."

Downhearted, Pete came out from under the bed and pulled on a pair of socks he'd found. They didn't match, except in odor.

Howie scampered out of the room before Pete could notice he was there.

Later that day, when there was no one in the house but Howie (except Bunnicula, who was sleeping), *it happened.*

A strange noise was coming from upstairs. *I'd better go investigate,* Howie thought.

Cautiously, the nervous but ever brave dachshund went up the stairs. With each step he took, the sound grew louder.

It's coming from Pete's room, he thought.

GA-RUNCH, CRRRUNNCHH, GA-RUM-RUM, GA-RUNCH!!!!

What was it?

The curious and daring Howie had to know.

The door creaked as he opened it.

The floor squeaked as he put one paw in front of another.

"Is someone there?" Howie asked. Even though he was trembling inside, his voice was as solid as a finely tuned concert piano.

"GA-RUNCH!" came the answer.

Howie's heart started racing. He dared not

move. He waited. He waited some more. He dozed off. He woke with a start.

That's when he heard the voice.

"Mo-o-o-re," it growled.

"M-M-More?" Howie asked.

"*MORE!*" it repeated.

The voice was coming from under the bed!

Howie moved at a snail's pace toward Pete's bed. He peered under it. Something was breathing, raspy and raw.

"Mo-o-o-re!" said the gravelly voice.

Howie thought his imagination was playing tricks on him. He wished there were someone else there to hear what he was hearing. He felt a lump in his throat as he thought of Delilah. He remembered her standing there with her picnic basket and little flag, calling him Johnny. He remembered her curly blonde ears and high-speed eyelashes.

Oh, Delilah, he thought.

But then he thought no more, for that was when he noticed the eyes staring out at him from under the bed.

The eyes were getting larger! Whoever they belonged to was coming toward him!

The formula! Howie thought.

He ran as fast as he could.

CHAPTER 7:
"THUMP, THUMP, THUMP!"

Howie bolted down the stairs. Whoever—or *whatever*—it was, was still coming after him! He could hear the *thump, thump, thump* of footsteps—or *whatever* they were—moving along the hallway over his head.

"Be brave, be brave," Howie told himself.

Suddenly, the footsteps—or *whatever* they were—stopped.

Howie looked up. There was nothing there.

And then . . . there it was!

It stood at the top of the stairs, raised on its hind legs, larger than Howie remembered it. *Much, much* larger.

PUDGYKINS!!!!

"Mo-o-o-re!" Pudgykins growled. "More food *now!!*"

As the overgrown koala started making its way awkwardly down the stairs, Howie glanced at the clock by the front door. It was too soon for any of the Monroes to come home. Bunnicula was asleep in the living room, and Harold and Chester were out somewhere. It was going to be up to him—Howie, the brave and courageous yet recently dumped and therefore heartbroken dachshund puppy—to save the day.

How much of a threat could a stuffed animal be? Howie asked himself.

Pudgykins stopped on the second step from the bottom, reached down, and picked up a sweatshirt lying there. It was Pete's and it still smelled like yesterday's soccer practice.

"Yum!" Pudgykins said as he stuffed the sweatshirt into his mouth.

Howie felt his knees buckle as he watched Pudgykins shred the sweatshirt with his sharklike teeth. In ten seconds the sweatshirt was nothing but a memory.

"Mo-o-o-re!" Pudgykins growled at Howie.

And then, before Howie's astonished eyes, Pudgykins began to swell. He grew taller and rounder and bigger. He was as big as Mr. Monroe now.

How long before he was as big as a house?

CHAPTER 8:
"IT ESCAPES!"

Howie did not wait to find out.

Being the heroic type he was, he would have waited, but after Pudgykins looked at him, licked his lips, and asked, "Got milk?" Howie thought it would be a good idea to find the nearest exit.

Once outside, he tried to think calmly. How to stop an overstuffed koala bear from achieving world domination? It was just the kind of question Chester would have loved. But where *was* Chester?

Suddenly, a new thought came into Howie's brain: Bunnicula!

The poor bunny was inside the house with Pudgykins! He, Howie the dauntless dachshund, would have to go back in and save him!!!!

He wished Delilah could be there to see him, then shook the thought out of his head.

Howie dashed back through the pet door, ready to do whatever it took to rescue the innocent bunny!

But Bunnicula was sound asleep in his cage, unharmed.

Whew, thought Howie, *Pudgykins hasn't found him yet.*

Then there was a loud CRASH!!!!!!

Oh, no! thought Howie. *Pudgykins has escaped!!!!!!*

Terrified screams confirmed Howie's hunch.

Passing the front closet on his way out, Howie noticed that all the Monroes' winter boots were missing.

Pudgykins has been here! Howie deduced smartly.

Out in the street, Howie was met with a sight too bewildering, too staggering, too weird for the human—or canine—mind to grasp. There, standing at the center of Maple and Elm, was a twenty-foot-tall koala bear picking up garbage pails and downing their contents as if they were nothing more than cans of soda.

"Food!" Pudgykins said between burps. "More!"

With every swallow, he grew another foot. High. Not at the end of his leg.

Howie's sharp and unusually large brain began to work overtime.

What could he do to save the world from Pete's terrible science experiment? He was only one small dachshund in a world gone mad, one tiny voice in a sea of voices, one pebble in a field of boulders, one itsy-bitsy minnow in a school of sharks, one

Howie's Writing Journal

Uncle Harold was just reading over my shoulder and said I'm getting a little carried away. He also wants to know why he and Pop aren't in the story. I told him I thought my readers wouldn't be too interested in such old characters.

Now he's not speaking to me, either.

A writer's life is a lonely life.

What could he do to save the world from Pete's terrible science experiment? He was only one small dachshund in a world gone mad. He might need to call in the army, the marines, the Humane Society. But how could he? His paws were too big to push the buttons on the phone!

Just then, the answer came to him, rounding the corner.

Pete! And who should Pete be walking with but Amber Faye Gorbish, Pete's classmate and—more important to the story—Delilah's owner.

Just the thought of Delilah made Howie's heart sink, but he refused to give in to sentiment. This was no time for romantic notions! This was a time for action!

Howie went bounding up to Pete, who said, "What's up, pup?"

"Woof!" Howie replied as he turned his handsome face with its chiseled profile up toward the towering koala bear, whom he would have thought was hard to miss.

"Pudgykins!" Pete cried. "How did you—"

And then an evil smile spread slowly across his face like an accident working its way across a carpet.

"The potion," Pete muttered. "It must have spilled onto Pudgykins. That means it works! It works, it works!"

"What potion? What are you talking about?" Amber Faye asked. "Pete, don't you see that there's a giant teddy bear blocking our way? What are you going to do about it?"

"No sweat!" Pete said. "Pudgykins is my bear. He'll do what I tell him."

"Cool," Amber Faye said, glancing at her watch. "But can he do it soon? Because if I am, like, one minute late for my piano lesson, my teacher will be, like, furious."

Amber Faye tossed her curly blonde hair the way Delilah had once tossed her curly blonde ears. *Like owner, like puppy,* Howie thought.

"PUDGYKINS!" Pete called out.

The giant koala bear, who was now taller than most of the trees, dropped the garbage pail it was holding and looked down at Pete. "Food!" it said.

"No, Pudgy, I'm not food. I'm your master. It's Pete, don't you remember?"

"Pete," Pudgykins repeated dully. He sounded one kibble short of a full meal. *Like owner, like teddy bear,* Howie thought.

By this time, quite a crowd had gathered. Even the police had showed up. Some of them were talking through megaphones, saying things like, "We've got you surrounded! Don't try any sudden moves! How's the weather up there?"

There were a lot of kids in the crowd, Toby Monroe among them, and pets, too. Howie spotted Harold and Chester and ran over to them.

"What's going on?" Harold asked the young but well-informed dachshund puppy.

Howie told them.

"*I* will save the day!" was Chester's response.

"Pete," Pudgykins kept saying. "Pete, Pete . . ."

Suddenly, a terrible smell overcame the crowd.

"P. U., what's that?" Howie heard someone say. He turned his head. To his surprise, the terrible smell was Delilah!

"Delilah!" he gasped. "Where have you been?"

Delilah's eyes were bleary. Her fur was matted. She had the lid of a pizza box stuck to her hind right paw. "I've been out at the town dump!" she snapped at Howie. "What's it to ya? I was drownin' my sorrows in trash."

"Sorrows?" Howie asked hopefully. Was Delilah's heart as broken as his own?

But before she could answer, Delilah was whisked out of sight!

Pudgykins had grabbed Delilah and was now holding her in his outstretched paw. His eyes gleamed as he looked at her and licked his chops. "Food!" he growled. "Yum."

HOWIE'S WRITING JOURNAL

I wonder what's going to happen next. Howie has to save Delilah, but how? Then again, since Delilah still isn't speaking to me, maybe I should just let Pudgykins . . .

Nah, that wouldn't be nice.

At least Uncle Harold is speaking to me again. He said he was just being too sensitive before. Besides, he wanted to read the rest of what I'd written. I let him. He said it was good, but that just because a simile works once doesn't mean you should use it again and again. I think he means the concert piano.

He also said I'm still overdoing the adjectives describing one of the characters.

I wish I knew what he was talking about.

Well, it's time to finish the story. In most stories like this, the monster has to be killed off. I like Pudgykins too much to kill him off. Besides, I am a gentle peace-loving creature and I do not want my story to be violent. How am I going to end this without blowing Pudgykins up?

Maybe the formula could wear off and he could grow small again.

Or maybe he could grow so big that he floats off into space and becomes another planet. Planet Pudgykins.

Maybe not.

I guess I'll just have to write it to find out what happens.

CHAPTER 9:
"HOWIE TO THE RESCUE!"

"Save me!" Delilah cried.

"Where's your boyfriend?" Howie cried back. "Why doesn't *he* save you?"

"I don't have a boyfriend!" Delilah sobbed. "I made that up. I couldn't stand worrying about you. You're *too* brave, *too* good, *too* smart, *too* strong—"

"Stop!" Howie shouted, even though he didn't really want her to. "I'll save you!"

Of course, to most people standing around,

the conversation sounded like this:

"Woof!" Delilah cried.

"Yip yip yip yip," Howie cried back. "Yip woof woof!"

"Whine whine yip yip woof!" Delilah sobbed. "Yip yip yip. Yip yip yip yip yip. Yip *woof* yip, *woof* yip, *woof* yip, *woof* yip—"

"Woof!" Howie shouted, even though he didn't really want her to. "Yip woof woof!"

The question was, *How* was Howie going to save Delilah? Why had Pudgykins picked her up in the first place? Except for that one moment when he'd eyed Howie as if he were snack food, the big Pudge seemed to have more of an attraction to smelly socks and old sweat-shirts and the contents of garbage pails and . . .

"That's it!" Howie cried. Delilah smelled

like garbage! That's why Pudgykins wanted to eat her! But she *wasn't* garbage. She was an innocent puppy who was the future mother of Howie's children.

Howie gasped. He couldn't believe he was thinking such a thing. It was true! He wanted to spend the rest of his life with Delilah! He wanted them to take long strolls along the beach together, sniffing for clams. He pictured them romping in the rain, sharing a laugh when the people they lived with complained later that they smelled like wet dogs. He saw them chasing pigeons in the village square as church bells chimed and . . .

"Howie!" Delilah called out. "Stop thinking so much and save me!"

"I will!" Howie called back. "I'll save you,

Delilah! Hang on! Don't let Pudgykins eat you!"

"That's good advice!" Delilah responded. "You're so smart and intelligent!"

"Get their sneakers!" Howie commanded Harold and Chester and several other pets who had gathered around and weren't being distracted by fire hydrants.

"Whose sneakers?" Chester asked.

"The kids' sneakers," Howie answered. "Now!"

Suddenly, all the kids in the crowd were being forced to give up their sneakers by dogs tugging at them and cats scratching at them.

"Say," said Police Officer Fogerty, "I think these animals are onto something here. The overgrown koala bear appears to like smelly things. It looks to me like that bright, fast-thinking wirehaired dachshund puppy is trying to get all the animals to get all the kids to take off their sneakers and fling them at the koala in order to save that beautiful but not very smart puppy hanging from the koala's clutches."

Howie thought, *I couldn't have put it better myself.*

"Come on, men!" the police officer went on. "Let's help them out!"

Before you could say "world domination," all the kids in the crowd were taking off their smelly sneakers and tossing them at Pudgykins. Unfortunately, because the koala was so big, most of the sneakers landed somewhere in the vicinity of his ankles.

"Get a fan!" Officer Fogerty commanded. "And a long extension cord!"

Before you could say "a finely tuned concert piano," all the sneakers were heaped in a huge pile and a fan was set up behind them.

"On!" Officer Fogerty shouted.

Someone flipped a switch, and the odor of a thousand gym classes wafted through the air. Several women and a couple of men fainted.

Howie looked up, his heart in his mouth.

(This is just an expression. Howie did not really have his heart in his mouth. This is not anatomically possible.)

Delilah was inches away from Pudgykin's open jaws. She was hanging there as limp as last month's lettuce.

"Pudgy!" Pete cried. "Look down here! Look

at the nice smelly sneakers we have for you!"

Just as the koala bear was about to partake of a morsel of dog, he turned his head and looked down at the crowd. Maybe it was the sound of Pete's voice. Or maybe the scent of sweaty feet had finally reached his nostrils.

Whatever it was, he slowly lowered the paw holding the delirious Delilah and reached out for the pile of sneakers. "Food!" he said. "Yum!"

As he began stuffing his mouth with Nikes and Adidas, as the crowd cheered, as church bells tolled and Officer Fogerty and his men shook one another's hands and slapped one another's backs, as the Red Cross revived the fallen few and the Society for the Prevention of Cruelty to Stuffed Animals arrived to

83

ensure that no harm would be done to any stuffed animals in the making of this book, as all the kids were shouting, "I always hated those sneakers, anyway!" and their parents were shouting, "If you think I'm going to run right out and buy you new sneakers just because some koala bear ate your old ones! . . . " As all this was going on, Howie ran to Delilah.

"Oh, Howie," she said, looking into his eyes the moment after she'd landed on the ground with a *ka-phlumph,* "you are my hero!"

"Marry me," Howie said, surprising even himself.

"But you think I'm beautiful but not very smart," Delilah said.

"I'm the one who's not very smart," said Howie.

"You're right," Delilah said with a laugh. "Oh, Howie, my Howie, yes, I will marry you."

Howie's knees buckled.

And they lived happily ever after.

THE END

HOWIE'S WRITING JOURNAL

Uncle Harold said, "What happened to Pudgykins?"

Oh. Right. Pudgykins.

CHAPTER 10:
"PUDGYKINS HELPS OUT"

After Pudgykins ate all the sneakers, Pete's brother, Toby, had a brilliant idea. "Instead of dominating the world," he said, "why doesn't Pudgykins *help* the world?"

"What a dorky idea," said Pete, who thought that world domination was the only cool thing worth going for.

But everyone else liked Toby's idea. They liked it so much that he got an A in science. (So did Pete.)

Pudgykins now lives on an island in the

middle of the ocean, where he eats most of the planet's garbage that is brought to him on many barges and he is single-handedly responsible for improving the quality of the ozone layer.

The only problem is that he keeps getting bigger.

Scientists from all over the world are working on it.

Including Pete Monroe.

THE END

Howie's Writing Journal

Uncle Harold is going to send my story to his editor!!!! He thinks it will be published!!!! I will be famous!!!!

Delilah said I am still too full of myself, but if I promised to make her smarter in my next story, she'd start speaking to me again. I promised. I might even make <u>her</u> the hero next time. I've got a literary license, so I can do whatever I want, right?

I just hope the editor lets me keep all those adjectives.